ANIMAL OLYMPICS

# The Jaguar
# and the Javelin

by A.H. Benjamin and Yuliya Somina

W
FRANKLIN WATTS
LONDON•SYDNEY

Franklin Watts
First published in Great Britain in 2016 by The Watts Publishing Group

ISBN 978 1 4451 4547 1 (hbk)
ISBN 978 1 4451 4549 5 (pbk)
ISBN 978 1 4451 4548 8 (library ebook)


**Series Editor:** Melanie Palmer
**Series Advisor**: Catherine Glavina
**Series Designer:** Peter Scoulding

Printed in China

Franklin Watts
An imprint of
Hachette Children's Group
Part of The Watts Publishing Group
Carmelite House
50 Victoria Embankment
London EC4Y 0DZ

An Hachette UK Company
www.hachette.co.uk

www.franklinwatts.co.uk

FSC
www.fsc.org
MIX
Paper from
responsible sources
FSC® C104740

Jaguar was good at sports. He had won lots of Olympic medals.

That's because Jaguar was fast ...

strong ...

agile ...

brave ...

... and so graceful!

Jaguar won medals at every sport. Except ...

7

... at the javelin. Jaguar couldn't get the hang of it ...

no matter how hard
he tried!

9

The javelin always flew
the wrong way.

"Watch out!" cried
the judges.

Jaguar was sure it was
the javelin's fault.

"I'll make my own,"
he said.

So he did. The first javelin flew to the right.

"Argh!" shrieked Parrot.

The second javelin went
left instead.

"Be careful!" shouted
Monkey.

Jaguar didn't see as he
threw his javelins about.

# They went everywhere!

Jaguar gave up.

He sat down.

"Javelins don't like me,"
he said, sadly.

Just then ...

"Help!" cried a voice.

It was Snake who had got himself tied into a knot.

# Jaguar soon untied him.

"Thank you," said Snake.
"Is there anything I can
do for you?"

"Er ... yes!" cried Jaguar.
"You look just right!"

He told Snake his idea.

A few days later, Jaguar won a gold medal. Snake was the perfect javelin!

# Puzzle 1

Put these pictures in the correct order.
Now tell the story in your own words.
How short can you make the story?

brave   lazy

fast

scared   worried

angry

Choose the words which best describe the characters. Can you think of any more? Pretend to be one of the characters!

# Answers

## Puzzle 1

The correct order is:

1d, 2f, 3b, 4a, 5e, 6c

## Puzzle 2

Jaguar     The correct words are brave, fast.
The incorrect word is lazy.

Judges     The correct words are scared, worried
The incorrect word is angry.

## Look out for more stories:

Robbie's Robot
ISBN 978 1 4451 3950 0 (HB)

The Green Machines
ISBN 978 1 4451 3954 8 (HB)

The Cowboy Kid
ISBN 978 1 4451 3946 3 (HB)

Dani's Dinosaur
ISBN 978 1 4451 3942 5 (HB)

Gerald's Busy Day
ISBN 978 1 4451 3934 0 (HB)

Billy and the Wizard
ISBN 978 0 7496 7985 9

The Frog Prince and the Kitten
ISBN 978 1 4451 1620 4

Bill's Scary Backpack
ISBN 978 0 7496 9468 5

Bill's Silly Hat
ISBN 978 1 4451 1617 4

Little Joe's Boat Race
ISBN 978 0 7496 9467 8

Little Joe's Horse Race
ISBN 978 1 4451 1619 8

Felix, Puss in Boots
ISBN 978 1 4451 1621 1

The Animals' Football Cup
ISBN 978 0 7496 9477 7

The Animals' Football Camp
ISBN 978 1 4451 1616 7

The Animals' Football Final
ISBN  978 1 4451 3879 4

That Noise!
ISBN 978 0 7496 9479 1

Cheeky Monkey's Big Race
ISBN 978 1 4451 1618 1

For details of all our titles go to: www.franklinwatts.co.uk